To: _____

From: _____

To my dad, who loved me as his own for forty years ~S.S.

For all the new pieces of the family puzzle: the little ones, the grown-ups, and the loving ones ~T.K.

Text copyright © 2024 by Little Tiger Press Ltd
Jacket art and interior illustrations copyright © 2024 by Tatiana Kamshilina

All rights reserved. Published in the United States by Doubleday, an imprint of
Random House Children's Books, a division of Penguin Random House LLC, New York.
Published simultaneously in the United Kingdom by Little Tiger Press, London, in 2024.

DOUBLEDAY YR with colophon is a registered trademark
of Penguin Random House LLC.

Visit us on the Web! rhcbooks.com

Educators and librarians, for a variety of teaching tools,
visit us at RHTeachersLibrarians.com

Library of Congress Cataloging-in-Publication Data
Names: Stansbie, Stephanie, author. | Kamshilina, Tatiana, illustrator.
Title: Always your stepdad / by Stephanie Stansbie ; illustrated by Tatiana Kamshilina.
Description: First American edition. | New York : Doubleday Books for Young Readers, [2024] |
Audience: Ages 3–7. | Summary: A celebration of the special bond between a stepfather and his stepchild.
Identifiers: LCCN 2023011841 (print) | LCCN 2023011842 (ebook) |
ISBN 978-0-593-70911-5 (trade) | ISBN 978-0-593-70912-2 (ebook)
Subjects: CYAC: Stories in rhyme. | Stepfathers—Fiction. | Family life—Fiction. |
LCGFT: Stories in rhyme. | Picture books.
Classification: LCC PZ8.3.S7875 Ak 2024 (print) | LCC PZ8.3.S7875 (ebook) | DDC [E]—dc23

MANUFACTURED IN CHINA
10 9 8 7 6 5 4 3 2 1
First American Edition

LTP/1400/5360/1023

Always Your Stepdad

By
Stephanie Stansbie

Illustrated by
Tatiana Kamshilina

Doubleday Books for Young Readers

The first day we met,
I was awkward and shy.
But your smile was
so warm and so wise.

How could I have known
how my life was to change
when I looked in those bright,
thoughtful eyes?

I'd missed your first steps
and your wobbly walk,
yet you took my whole heart
in your hand.

You guided me gently along this new path.
It was me who was learning to stand!

When strangers would tell us,
"You're both so alike!"

I felt joyful and proud to my core.

All those times . . . dressing up,

playing cards,

MOVIE PASS
SUNFLOWER TREASURE
★ ★ ★ ★ ★

watching films,

how I cheered you up
when you felt sad.

So now, hand in hand,
through all weathers together,
you know you have nothing to fear.

TRAIN TICKET

KET

You're more precious to me
than I could have dreamed.

And I promise . . .

...I'll always be here.